FOR ERICA
(FLYING SOLO ISN'T SO SCARY AFTER ALL)

I HAVE ALWAYS BEEN FASCINATED BY EVERYTHING ELIZABETHAN:
THE CLOTHES, THE MUSIC, THE DANCING, THE FOOD. WHEN I HAD THE
IDEA FOR A STORY ABOUT A YOUNG BOY WHO IS FLUNG THROUGH TIME
TO LAND ON THE STAGE OF THE GLOBE THEATRE IN TUDOR LONDON,
I SAW MY CHANCE TO SHARE THOSE HARSH, DIRTY, BRUTAL, BEAUTIFUL
TIMES WITH OTHERS. I MADE MY WAY THROUGH A MOUNTAIN OF BOOKS
TO DISCOVER ALL THE AMAZING HISTORICAL DETAILS OF THE ERA; THEN
I DRAFTED AND REDRAFTED THE STORY TO MAKE IT RICH AND REAL.

ONE OF THE THINGS I LEARNED WAS THAT SHAKESPEARE'S PLAYS WERE
PERFORMED AT FOUR O'CLOCK ON MIDSUMMER AFTERNOONS. THAT WAS
WHEN I KNEW I HAD THE KEY TO THE MAGIC IN THIS BOOK.

GREGORY ROGERS

The BOY · The BEAR
The BARON · The BARD

Gregory Rogers

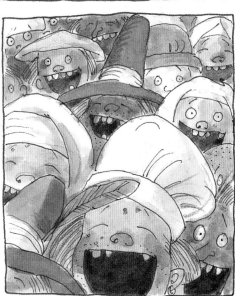

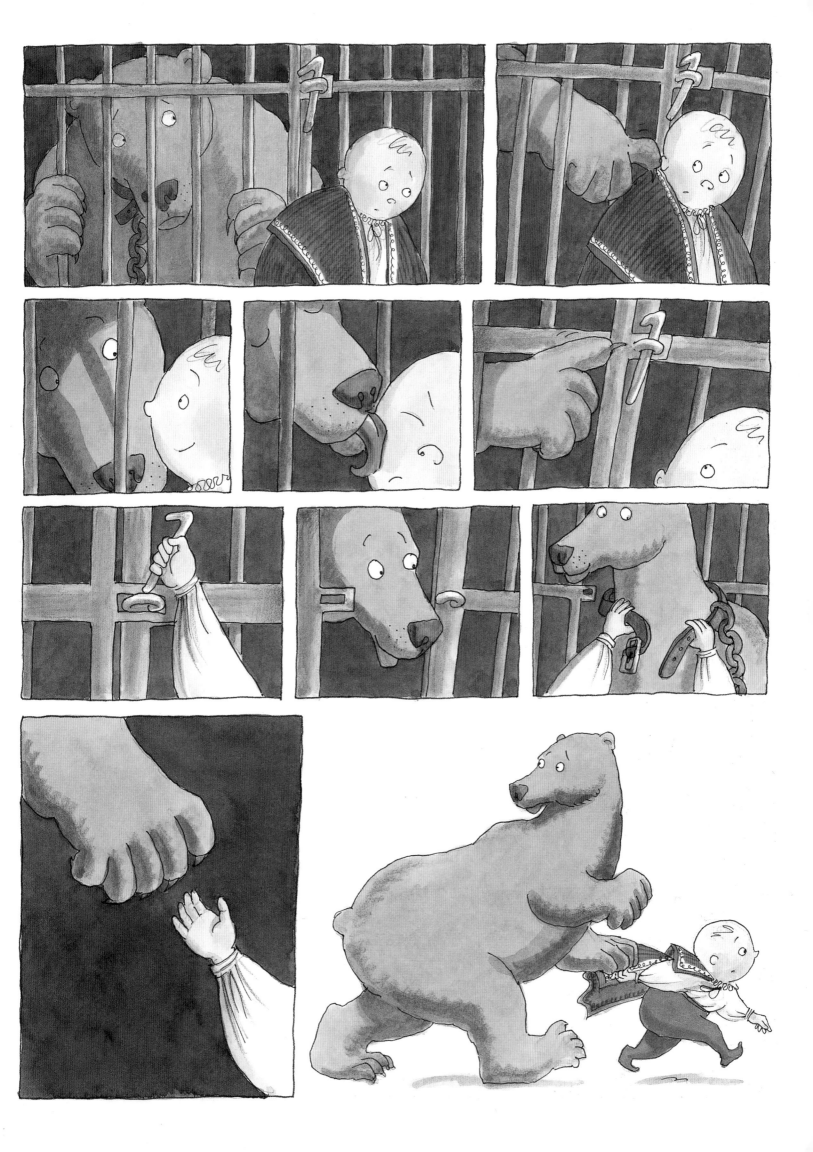

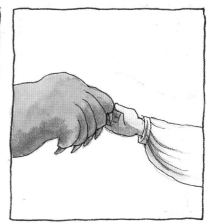

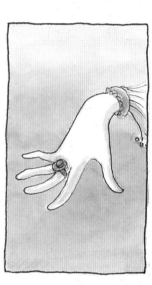

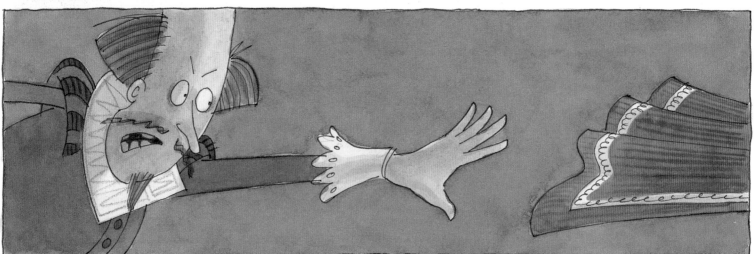

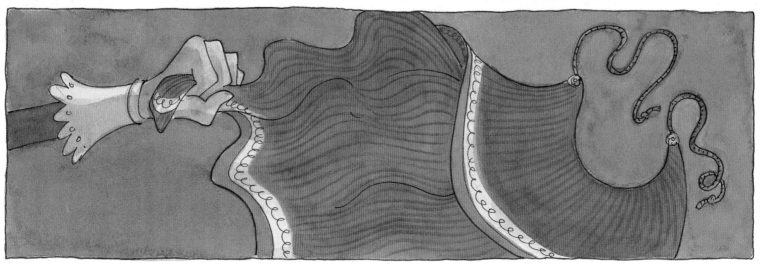

ACKNOWLEDGEMENTS

I want to thank all those people who helped me to make this book a reality. Thanks Jenny Thynne for your help with all things British, Margaret Connolly for being the best agent in the world and Jodie Webster for your keen eye that can spot a fumble at fifty paces. Thanks Neal Porter for showing faith in the new kid on the block. And thanks to my supporters on the home front, Bart, Harry and Pudding.

First published in 2004
This edition published in 2008

Allen & Unwin
83 Alexander Street
Crows Nest NSW 2065
Australia
Phone: (61 2) 8425 0100
Fax: (61 2) 9906 2218
Email: info@allenandunwin.com
Web: www.allenandunwin.com

National Library of Australia
Cataloguing-in-Publication entry:

Rogers, Gregory, 1957- .
The boy, the bear, the baron, the bard.

For children.
ISBN 978 1 74114 535 9 (PBK.).

I. Title. (Series: Rogers, Gregory, 1957 Boy bear series; 1).

A823.4

Cover design by Sandra Nobes
Printed in China by Everbest Printing Co. Ltd

1 3 5 7 9 10 8 6 4 2

GREGORY ROGERS studied fine art at Queensland College of Art and worked as a graphic designer before taking up freelance illustration. He was the first Australian to be awarded the prestigious Kate Greenaway Medal. *The Boy, the Bear, the Baron, the Bard* was first published in Australia in 2004 where it was short-listed for several awards including an Australian & New Zealand Illustration Award. It has also been published in the UK, France, the Netherlands and the USA, where it received critical acclaim including a selection as a Notable Children's Book of the Year for the American Library Association. Its sequel *Midsummer Knight* was published in Australia and internationally. It was a Notable Book in the Children's Book Council Awards, Younger Readers, 2007.

Gregory lives in Brisbane, Australia. He shares a dusty old, crowded house with his partner and two cats.

BOOK 2

MIDSUMMER KNIGHT

Midsummer Knight is a swashbuckling story of friendship and courage.

On a morning of midsummer magic, the Bear discovers an enchanted world in the heart of the forest. But there is treachery at work and the Bear is swept up in a sinister plot that lands him in the palace dungeons. After masterminding a crafty escape he leads his new friends into a royal battle – but what hope do they have once swords are drawn?

An irresistible companion to the internationally acclaimed *The Boy, the Bear, the Baron, the Bard.*